The Perfect Tea Party

Adapted by Andrea Posner-Sanchez
Based on the script "Tea for Too Many" by Doug Cooney
Illustrated by Grace Lee

❤ A GOLDEN BOOK • NEW YORK

ISBN 978-0-7364-3109-5
randomhouse.com/kids
Printed in the United States of America
10 9 8 7 6 5 4 3 2 1

It's an exciting day at Royal Prep—the fairies are choosing which student will host the annual school tea party.

Sofia's new stepsister, Amber, explains that Royal Prep tea parties are really big events. "They have merry-go-rounds, ponies, and even hot-air balloons!"

Sofia has never been to a royal tea party. She just recently became a princess when her mother married King Roland.

In class, Sofia's teacher, Flora, holds out a teapot. "Only students who haven't had a chance to host a party should submit their names," says the fairy.

Sofia excitedly drops a slip of paper with her name on it into the teapot.

Flora uses her wand to stir the pot. Soon one paper magically floats out.

"The host of the next Royal Prep tea party will be . . . Princess Sofia!" she announces.

Sofia is thrilled.

"You can throw any kind of party you like," Flora tells her. "This is your chance to show us who you are."

Sofia

On the ride home from school, Sofia talks about the tea party with Amber and her stepbrother, James. "There have already been so many big, fancy tea parties," she says. "I'd like to throw a simple tea party like I used to in the village. My friends and I would spread blankets on the ground and borrow teacups from our mothers."

James thinks that sounds cool. Amber doesn't. "No one wants to use borrowed teacups!" she exclaims. "When it comes to royal parties, the bigger the better!"

Sofia starts to think that maybe Amber is right. She spots the swan fountain and tells Baileywick, the castle caretaker, that she would like to have a swan-themed tea party. "We'll have swan-shaped cookies and cakes."

"That sounds lovely," says Baileywick. Amber likes the swan theme but encourages Sofia to think even bigger.

"Hmm. Maybe Cedric, the Royal Sorcerer, can make the tables and chairs float in the air like swans float on water," suggests Sofia. "And the swans can put on a show."

"That's more like it!" says Amber.

Later that day, Sofia is visited by her friends from the village, Jade and Ruby. Even though Sofia is busy planning the Royal Prep tea party, she is happy to take a break to spend time with them.

"Let's have a little snack," Sofia suggests. "I know the perfect spot."

Sofia leads Jade and Ruby along a row of hedges. Then she pushes aside some ivy, uncovering a wooden door. The door opens and the girls step into Sofia's secret garden.

"It's beautiful!" says Ruby.

"Look at all the butterflies!" cries Jade.

The girls spread out a blanket and share a plate of cookies. "This reminds me of the tea parties we had in the village," Ruby says. "Are you throwing a party like this for your princess friends?"

Sofia sighs. "I want to, but they expect a big, fancy tea party."

"That's too bad, because I'm having a great time just doing this," says Ruby.

"Me too," agrees Sofia.

After a few more cookies, Sofia sadly says good-bye and gets back to her party planning.

"Ah, Princess Sofia, you're just in time to choose the plates for your party," Baileywick says as Sofia enters the dining room.

Sofia looks at all the choices. She likes the simple white ones.

Amber shakes her head and holds up a large, shiny golden plate. "You need something like this," she declares. "Remember, bigger is better."

Sofia gives in and agrees to use the large golden plates.

At another table, James is happily munching on a swan-shaped cookie. "These are great!" he declares as crumbs fall from his mouth.

"You should order two hundred of these cookies for the tea party, and make them as big as possible," Amber tells Sofia. "You'll need a huge swan cake, too!"

Sofia thinks it's too much, but she listens to Amber anyway.

Next, Sofia heads to Cedric's workshop.
"I'm hosting a tea party tomorrow, and it would
be great if you could make all the tables and chairs
rise just a little bit off the ground,"
Sofia explains to the Royal
Sorcerer. "Do you have a
spell that can do that?"

Floaticus - hover - a - boo!

Cedric points his wand at a beaker on his worktable. "Floaticus-hover-a-boo!" The beaker twinkles magically and rises into the air.

"That's terrific!" cries Sofia. "See you at the party tomorrow."

Sofia goes to the swan fountain. Luckily, the magical amulet King Roland gave her, the Amulet of Avalar, gives her the power to talk to animals!

"I'm hosting a tea party, and I was hoping you could perform a water ballet," she tells the swans.

"It would be our pleasure," replies Portia.

"Great! See you tomorrow!" says Sofia, and rushes off to find the perfect tea party dress.

As the royal dressmaker hems her gown, Sofia tells her
mother about the tea party. "It is going to be so big and fancy.
Amber says everyone is going to love it." She sighs. "But part of
me wishes I could just have a sweet tea party like the ones I used
to have with Ruby and Jade."

"I'm sure everyone will be pleased no matter what kind of
party you throw," says Queen Miranda.

The day of Sofia's royal tea party has arrived! As the servants rush about, everything goes wrong. The swan-shaped ice sculpture falls off its cart and slides into the baker, who drops his tray of swan cookies. Then the ice slides into the fountain, scaring the swans.

The swans fly into Cedric just as he is casting his floating spell! The tables and chairs rise off the ground—and float away! Sofia can't believe her eyes!

The princess regrets listening to Amber. Her party is ruined, and the guests are on their way. Sofia starts to cry. Then she spots a butterfly and knows exactly what to do.

When the students and fairies arrive, Baileywick moves aside some ivy, pushes open the wooden door, and welcomes them into Sofia's secret garden. Blankets on the grass have been set with teapots and cups. Butterflies flutter over the flowers. And all the princesses love it—including Amber!

"Nice job, Sofia! I guess bigger isn't always better," Amber admits.

"Princess Sofia, what a charming party!" Flora tells the hostess. "Some peppermint tea, a pretty garden, and a beautiful view. Who could ask for more?"

All the guests raise their teacups and cheer, "To Princess Sofia!"

Sofia is pleased to learn that even princesses can enjoy simple things. She giggles and raises her own teacup. "Hooray for me!"